# WHAT HAPPENED TO THE ORANGES?

# WHAT HAPPENED TO THE ORANGES?

*Whispers Before the Scream*

*Fifteen Stories of Quiet Defiance*

Tiffany Higgins

© 2025 Tiffany Higgins

All rights reserved.

No part of this publication may be reproduced, stored in a retrieval system, or transmitted in any form or by any means—electronic, mechanical, photocopying, recording, or otherwise—without prior written permission from the author.

This is a work of fiction. Names, characters, places, and incidents are products of the author's imagination or used fictitiously. Any resemblance to actual events, locales, or persons, living or dead, is purely coincidental.

Published by Tiffany Higgins

Cover design, formatting, and trailer by the author.

ISBN: 9798292141136

First Print edition: August 2025

# *These stories are for you.*

*You with lived truths—whispered in the dark, shared with the world, or simply lived. Your defiance is not for nothing. You are among the survivors.*

*You carry your stories with you, challenge the systems, and stand up with a gentle integrity. You are seen.*

*And, if these pages echo something you have lived, you are not alone.*

*What Happened to the Oranges?*

# TABLE OF CONTENTS

Who is Lolly-Ann?..................................................................3

A City to Call Home..............................................................7

A Job's a Job............................................................................13

Civilized Dining....................................................................19

And Then She Came Knocking... ....................................23

Shattered Screams................................................................27

The Mischief Echoes............................................................37

War on Foreign Soil.............................................................41

The Visitor .............................................................................43

Dawn's Early Light..............................................................45

In the Woods ........................................................................49

Chocolate Sundae, No Tomato .......................................57

Two Stuffies Walk into a Bar ...........................................63

On the Tip of the Tongue ..................................................71

What Happened to the Oranges? ...................................73

About Tiffany .......................................................................75

More by Tiffany Higgins ...................................................77

*What Happened to the Oranges?*

# I.

Sometimes you're on your own.

Tiffany Higgins

*What Happened to the Oranges?*

## WHO IS LOLLY-ANN?

> *She didn't disappear—she simply chose to be where the world couldn't define her.*

She didn't want to be like everybody else—she wanted to be Lolly-Ann. Everywhere she went, somebody had an idea of what that should mean. But why should she care what they thought? After all, she was Lolly-Ann, not them.

Back in school, because she had good grades, her teachers and guidance counselor thought she should go to college—and get good grades there, too. Her father, a psychiatrist, had raised her to be true to herself—but he'd always expected her to follow in his footsteps.

Her mother, the spoiled sort, had been certain that Lolly-Ann would come to enjoy life as a stay-at-home wife. She'd dreamed of shopping trips and long lunches—spending too much, eating too little. Even her friends had pulled her in every direction.

Really, they were the reason she gave herself the graduation gift she did. After all, she just wanted a bit of time to herself. Some space to think. And who was going to give her that at home? Absolutely nobody. That's who. So, she booked a small site at a campground inside a national park.

Every morning was crisp, and her thoughts were the clearest they'd ever been. She crawled out of her tent and breathed deep, lungs filling with clean nature. After coaxing the fire back to life, she'd percolate her coffee. You haven't had coffee until you've tasted it percolated over an open flame.

It was those views, coffee in hand, that had probably sealed her fate. Trees stretched as far as her eye could see, with paths disappearing deep into the forest. The campground was tidy and nestled into the land to disturb nature as little as possible.

That week, Lolly-Ann fell in love — with the landscape, the gentle quiet, and the scent of pine and campfire. The worst part was packing up to leave. She stopped by the office to check out of her campsite. The clerk bustled in, clearly frazzled.

"I'm sorry," he said, looking genuinely apologetic. "Guy just up and quit on me. Said he found love with one of the campers. Climbed into a van full of people, and — gone. I don't suppose you're looking for a job."

He was probably joking — but her curiosity go the better of her. Turned out, it was exactly what she was looking for. The job came with a small cabin and shared kitchen access. The pay wasn't terrible — but what sold her was the promise of unlimited nature, on and off the clock.

Lolly-Ann said yes, right then and there. No haggling — what he offered felt fair. She checked out the cabin, left some of her gear. Promised she'd be back within a week — then headed home to break the news to everyone who'd already decided her future.

## *What Happened to the Oranges?*

She'd worked as a campground clerk for over a decade—tending both campers and the grounds. The clerk who'd hired her had become her husband. Now, they lived in a big family cabin, with a couple of tots underfoot. Neither could imagine leaving nature behind—not for the crowded towns or the bustling cities they came from.

Tiffany Higgins

*What Happened to the Oranges?*

## A City to Call Home

> *Some cities welcome you. Others require you to disappear before you can belong.*

She turned another corner. Nothing looked familiar—but everything looked the same.

She wasn't going to panic. She absolutely refused. Panic was setting in.

Why had she moved here? What in the name of all the gods had convinced her to choose this overpacked city—swarming with a million and one citizens? The buildings were practically on top of each other. Had they all been printed from the same 3D printer?

She took a deep breath. Was that man following her? In a city this crowded, it was hard to tell. Everyone pressed forward—dressed the same, moving in unison. It was unnerving.

Where had she parked? It had to be nearby. She turned another corner.

Was he still following? Had he been wearing a hat before, or was it her imagination?

She reminded herself: she'd landed her dream job. It was everything she'd been looking for. She chose her hours. Her clients. She even had her own office. The only catch had been the move.

She'd accepted the position on one condition: they find a comfortable place that she and her 4-year-old daughter could truly call home. And they had delivered—a spacious, sunlit apartment near a neighborhood park.

Would she ever find her way back—back to her car, her apartment, her beautiful daughter waiting at home with her new sitter? She turned another corner. That man had definitely followed her.

She darted into traffic—horns blaring, brakes squealing--but didn't stop until she'd reached the safety of the far sidewalk. Breath hitching, she turned. The creep was gone. Swallowed by the throng.

She turned and melted into the crowd. There had been a coffee shop across from the parking structure—but which one? There was a clone on nearly every corner.

She ducked into the first shop she spotted—needing coffee and a safe place to gather her thoughts. The bored teenager behind the counter barely glanced up.

Armed with the largest coffee they had and an intimidating-looking bear claw, she settled into a table in the corner. One bite, and she began to relax—the flavors melted over her tongue. Maybe the city wasn't all bad.

She fished her phone from her pocket, dug out the parking stub from her purse, and punched the garage into her map. Only a few blocks away.

## *What Happened to the Oranges?*

She finished the last cinnamony sweet bite, tossed her trash in the receptacle, grabbed her coffee, and finally headed toward her car. The setting sun painted the glass buildings in hues of orange and pink. For the first time, she saw the city was truly beautiful.

Tiffany Higgins

# II.

Ethics are tested. Lines are blurred.

Tiffany Higgins

## A Job's a Job

*Some jobs steal your soul quietly. Others force you to write ransom notes.*

I stared at the screen, impatient. What was I supposed to write? It wasn't like I'd done this before.

"Where do I begin? Where do you think I should begin?" I asked my guest.

"Hrmp errm armph…"

"That can't be right."

"Hgga ermppa oomp…"

"If you're going to be rude, maybe just keep your mouth shut?"

Next came the clattering of the chair legs. The ruckus was obnoxious. My guest's welcome already wearing thin.

"I'll just do it myself," I declared and returned to my keyboard. He slammed the chair harder, destroying my concentration. I stood, walked over, and punched him in the face. He crumpled, slumping against the chair. Silence. I returned to my seat.

"Now, where was I? Ah, yes. Your ransom. How much do you think you're worth?"

He didn't answer.

"Nothing, huh? You're probably right."

My laughter bounced off the walls, echoing back hollow and sharp. Still, that ransom note hadn't written itself, and I was going to have to do it.

"Dear Sir or Madam," I typed.

Too formal. Too impersonal. Delete. Start over.

"If you ever want to see your beloved Jimmy again." That was better. "Then follow the instructions precisely. If you should stray from the course, then your loved one will suffer the consequences."

I heard the sound of groaning behind me. The guest of honor was stirring. I tapped the disk icon to save my work. I brought myself to stand in front of my guest again.

"Gnkt hikgt mbb."

"We gonna have a problem?"

"Mmm mmm, mmm mmm." He shook his head emphatically.

"Sit there quietly and don't make a sound. Can you do that?"

He nodded agreeably. All the fight had drained out of him. I raised my hand. He flinched. I patted him gently on the cheek. He whimpered.

I returned again to the ransom note. It was nearly perfect. It was only missing one detail. I turned in my chair.

"If I remove the gag, are you going to scream, shout, and yell? Because no one will hear you. You will only succeed in pissing me off. You've already seen what happens when you piss me off. You don't want me to hit you again, do you?"

## *What Happened to the Oranges?*

He shook his head. Keeping my temper in check, I removed the gag.

"Look, man… I think you have the wrong guy. I'm a nobody. Nobody cares enough to pay for me, and I don't have a penny to my name."

"Bullshit," I spat. "I saw your apartment. Took you from yor bed."

He started laughing—a loud sort of guffaw of laughter. I lifted an eyebrow and waited.

"Dude that lives there's my buddy. He's outta town. I've been crashing there—squatting, really. He doesn't even know."

I raised the other eyebrow.

"Check the photos. Not one has me in it. Go see for yourself if you don't believe me."

I put the gag back on. I scrubbed my hands over my face. I felt my frustration returning. I grabbed the chair and dragged him toward the closet. He protested.

"Shut up!"

He obeyed. Blessed silence. I stuffed him in the closet. A closet I'd reinforced for exactly this. I closed the door and secured it with a padlock. The padlock featured a word lock. A word that I'd chosen myself.

E-E-R-F would free him.

I leaned against the door. I could hear the muffled sounds of movement. He wasn't attempting escape—just shifting, settling into his restraints.

Wrong guy? Was it possible? I shook off the feeling of dread as I returned to the ransom note. All I had to do was write a few instructions to be followed. Once the ransom had been paid, I'd collect my fee and be on my way.

The instructions were simple, almost friendly. Just enough to make them feel watched, even if no one was there.

Along the way, they would collect a key to a locker down at Central Station. Inside that locker, they would find a laptop supplied by my employer. With the laptop, they would uncover the final instructions for paying the ransom. I printed the note.

My employer had supplied me with an old-fashioned Polaroid camera. I loaded it and returned to the closet.

"E." I scrolled the first tumbler into place.

"E." Then the second.

"R." The third tumbler clicked.

"F." The lock slid free.

I opened the door. His eyes were pleading. His face streaked with tears. He made no sound.

The old camera whirred, mechanical and loud. I smiled. New tech never delivers sound like that. I leaned against the door jam while I awaited the final exposure.

Jimmy–at least, I hoped it was Jimmy–faded slowly into view. The tears came last, blooming like bruises as the image set.

"Perfect," I said as I closed the door and resecured the padlock.

## *What Happened to the Oranges?*

I snatched the paper from the printer tray. I tri-folded the note with the image at its center. I slid it into an envelope and sealed it with a damp sponge.

The doorbell rang. I'd finished my missive just in time. My employer had sent a messenger to collect the ransom note and deliver it to the family.

I tidied up the borrowed home. On a Post-it, I scrawled: E-E-R-F. I stuck it to the closet door. I took one last look around, gathered up the few items I'd brought with me, and slipped into the garage.

Ten minutes later, I was flying down the coastal highway toward my favorite burger shack. With my part of the job finished, there was nothing left to do but wait for the ka-ching sound my phone would make when the payment arrived in my bank account.

# Tiffany Higgins

*What Happened to the Oranges?*

# CIVILIZED DINING

*Some appetites require restraint.*

🍊🍊🍊

Johnathon put on the prison guard uniform, then turned to the mirror. He smoothed out the fabric, each motion revealing the bulge and ripple of muscle beneath the cheap polyester fabric.

It had taken him years to grow accustomed to his lack of reflection. For the better part of a century, he'd avoided mirrors altogether. Until one night at a tavern, when a rude boy snidely remarked to a friend.

"Doesn't the poor chap even own a mirror?" the boy jeered. His friend bellowed with laughter.

Johnathon had drained them both as they stumbled home that night. He found a mirror soon after—and realized what a slovenly mess he'd become. He learned to accept that he'd never see his own face again.

Uniform set, boots strapped, he stepped out of the bedroom, and snatched his keys off the counter. He was whistling on his way out. He was hungry.

The drive was short. He eased into a parking space and stared through the windshield at the cold, gray hulk of the prison. The sky, as always, hovered on the edge of rain.

His teeth flashed—the vampire equivalent of a stomach growl. He wondered what was on the menu tonight.

"Dovin," he greeted the gate guard with a nod.

"Johnathon," the man replied, swinging the gate open.

Screaming broke out across the yard. Johnathon raised an eyebrow at Dovin, who only shrugged.

"I'd better see what the ruckus is about."

His boots thudded against the ground as he ran toward the screams. He shoved through the doors, sprinted down the corridor, and burst into the cafeteria just as the screaming rose again. Five pairs of eyes snapped to him.

Three men in prison orange huddled in a corner, hands raised. On the floor, Vinnie Mandeecio writhed and screamed. Vinnie had a rap sheet a mile long—but it was all petty. A month here, a year there, always out again and mixed up in something new.

The fifth set of eyes belonged to fellow guard Kenny McGuire—beyond ravenous, barely holding control. The air was tinged with copper. Vinnie must have injured himself.

"Shit," Johnathon muttered, moving in to stop what was already unraveling.

He stepped between McGuire and Vinnie. His fangs flashed—hunger twisting inside him. He shoved it down. This wasn't the civilized way.

"McGuire!" he barked. "Stop. Mandeecio's an innocent."

"Yeah, yeah—I was framed. It wasn't me. Really," Vinnie whined.

## *What Happened to the Oranges?*

McGuire's fangs gleamed. He hadn't fed properly in days. Angry, twitchy, starving. These prisoners had the misfortune of pulling cleanup duty with this idiot guarding them.

Johnathon's fangs slid out—smooth, patient. He was older, stronger, more disciplined. McGuire? All headstrong self-confidence.

"Take your friend and go," Johnathon said over his shoulder.

The three prisoners hauled Vinnie toward the back door. McGuire lurched after them, reaching for the Vinnie.

"No," McGuire growled. "You three can go—but leave Mandeecio." He licked his lips. "I can already taste him."

Johnathon seized McGuire's shoulders.

"Damnit McGuire. Not this way. It's not the way—not anymore."

The young vampire swung—Johnathon dodged without effort.

"What's the difference, whether it's Mandeecio or Welforg?"

"Welforg's a filthy coward—murdered innocent kids so they couldn't tell what he did to 'em."

The doors slammed shut behind the escaping men. Johnathon hoped they'd take Vinnie to the infirmary. McGuire still fumed—but didn't follow.

"How long've you been turned?" Johnathon asked.

"Six months, maybe. I was sick—probably dying. My wife had this… 'friend.' Now here I am. And I've never been so hungry my damn life."

"I remember the hunger," Johnathon said quietly. Then he slung an arm around McGuire's shoulders. "Come on—let's go see if Welforg's on the menu tonight."

He led McGuire out the doors opposite the fleeing men. Welforg sounded like the perfect cure for the hunger burning in them both.

*What Happened to the Oranges?*

# AND THEN SHE CAME KNOCKING...

*Character writing can be intense and, sometimes, all too real.*

Her husband had taken the kids on a fishing trip with their grandfather. She relished a weekend of peace. It seemed the perfect opportunity to start her newest novel.

She poured herself a cup of coffee and sank into the comfiest chair in the house. As she sipped, she fired up her laptop. Soon, the clacking of keys filled the room.

> *Sun blazed in the summer sky. She glared at the yellow orb impairing her vision. A pearl of sweat traced her temple and slipped into her ear. She tipped her sun hat and lifted a hand to shield her eyes. The kids kicked the ball from one end of the field to the other and then back again.*

**Knock. Knock. Knock.**

"Damn it," she muttered, setting her laptop aside.

She grabbed her purse, expecting a neighbor kid with candy bars, wrapping paper, or some other fundraiser. She hoped it was cookie dough—the one fundraiser she looked forward to.

"What are we selli—" Her words caught in her throat. A woman stood on the porch.

The sun—a white-hot halo behind her—was just as blinding as the one she'd been writing about. That had to be it. That's why the woman was a dead ringer for her character.

"Help me. Please. They're after me."

The woman pushed past her, stumbling into the house and not stopping until she reached the living room.

The room was cozy—overstuffed couch, matching chairs, coffee table, end tables, a modest TV on the wall. Her laptop waited beside a cup of cooling coffee.

The woman paced. There wasn't much space, but she made it work—tight turns, anxious energy. She slipped her phone from her pocket, thumb hovering over the screen. Time to call the police.

**No Service** blinked on the screen.

She tried to recall the last time service had dropped. Never—not here. Maybe the laptop would work.

**No Service** glared from the laptop's screen—bold, unmistakable, visible from across the room.

"Who's after you?" she asked at last, eyes tracking the woman's restless path.

The police were clearly off the table. She needed to figure out what she was dealing with—and for a flicker of a moment, she wished she'd gone on that fishing trip after all.

The woman's sun hat was tilted—just like the one she'd imagined. A bright pink sundress, scattered with large white flowers, flowed around her knees. The exact dress her new character wore.

Blonde waves hung down her back. Instinct whispered that in the light, copper threads would flicker through. And, those neon flip-flops? The final, impossible detail.

She'd planned to use the flip-flops as a small quirk—maybe a teenage daughter would roll her eyes every time her mom wore those awful green sandals. She hadn't decided yet how that detail would land.

The woman caught her staring. "Oh—my daughter hates them. Probably why I wore them today. I was at her soccer game. That's when I saw them."

She turned to the window. Sunlight glinted off the copper strands in her hair.

"Who? Who did you see?"

"The men. There."

She pointed to a nondescript black sedan parked down the street. Maybe someone was inside—but the sun on the windshield turned it to mirrored glass. The woman resumed pacing—tight, sharp turns as if trying to outwalk whatever haunted her.

"What brought you here?" she asked, her voice quieter now— more wary than curious.

"I don't know. I just… knew. If I knocked on that door, someone would answer. And that someone would help me."

"How can I help you?"

"I don't know. I just followed my gut—and here I am."

She glanced out the window. The sun was sinking fast, painting the sky in orange streaks with pink trailing at the edges.

"They're gone," she whispered, eyes wide.

The car sat: empty and silent. The woman's pacing quickened, her agitation growing as rapidly as the shadows stretching across the room. A crash shattered the quiet—somewhere at the back of the house.

"They're here!" the woman shouted, bolting for the stairs.

She froze, watching the woman take the stairs three at a time. Follow the stranger into her family's private space? Or investigate the crash from the back of the house?

Something slammed into the back of her head. Vision clouded. She crumpled to the floor. She thought she heard boots pounding on hardwood as the world turned black.

*What Happened to the Oranges?*

## SHATTERED SCREAMS

*She wrote thrillers until the night she became part of one.*

She's wearing a pair of charcoal-colored leggings and an oversized, fuzzy sweater in hues of browns and blues. Her blue knit socks are scrunched at the ankles. She's cocooned in a toasty afghan her grandmother crocheted long ago. A coffee sits on the side table—forgotten, steam a fading memory.

She sits by the window. Snow has been falling all day. She hasn't noticed. The sun is fading, and she absentmindedly turns on the lamp beside her. She clicks and clacks at the keys of her laptop which is balanced precariously on her lap. It wobbles as she shifts in her seat. Excitement thrums in her veins—her story is racing toward its climax.

The heroine of her story had just arrived face to face with the serial killer who'd meticulously eliminated every one of her friends. She was breathing heavily as she prepared for the inevitable showdown.

**POP!**

The power cuts out. The laptop glows too brightly, throwing eerie shadows into the sudden dark.

"Shit!"

She checks the battery icon—when had she last charged it? Quickly, she saves the file to her hard drive. Then to the thumb drive. No cloud without power. She leaves the lid up, letting the soft glow light her search for candles.

**Thump, thump, thud.**

From the kitchen? She closes the drawer, still candleless, and pats her pockets. No phone. Probably left it in the kitchen—like always.

**Whoosh, thud, thud, thump.**

She grabs the fire poker and exhales once. Then slips into the kitchen doorway, squinting into the dark, scanning for shadows that don't belong.

She makes out the hulking shape of the refrigerator across the room. Moonlight creeps from behind thick grey clouds, just enough to kiss the edge of the sink. The door is closed tight—no light slips through.

**Schwump, thump, thud.**

She cocks her head and holds her breath. Listens—to the silence, and for something breathing back. Her heartbeat is thunder, drowning out everything else.

She slides her feet skatelike across the floor to the counter. She feels around for her phone. It isn't there.

**Schwump, whoosh, thud.**

Louder? Closer? Inside the kitchen? Just outside the door?

## *What Happened to the Oranges?*

Her heartbeat roars in her ears now, louder with every second. Panic blooms. She grips the fire poker tighter—had she forgotten she held it?

She raises it over her shoulder like a baseball bat as she skates across the floor towards the door.

**Whoosh, thump, schwump.**

Someone is outside the door. That somebody who killed the power to her house—way out here. Late. Dark. Isolated.

"Oh hell no!" she shouts, flings the door open, and plants her feet like a batter at the plate.

**Whoosh, schwump, splat.**

A pile of snow slides from the roof, landing at her feet and spilling across her kitchen floor. She stands frozen as cold seeps through her socks and into her bones.

She drops the fire poker. It clatters against tile. Laughter bubbles up—deep, primal, ridiculous.

She stands in the puddling snow, laughing as cold air whips through the open door and slaps her rosy.

**Whoosh, schwump, splat.**

Another pile of snow hits the floor. She shuts the door, turns the lock, and peels off her soaked socks as she returns to the counter.

**Whoosh, thump, thud.** The falling pile of snow barely registers this time.

She reaches blindly through the odds-and-ends drawer near the end of the counter. Her fingers close around something candle-shaped—broken in the middle, but good enough.

Though she doesn't allow smoking in the house, she always keeps a book of matches in an ashtray on the kitchen table. She feels her way through the dark kitchen toward it.

"Son of a..." she stubs her toe on a kitchen chair.

She gropes across the table, searching for the ashtray—but finds her phone instead. She taps the power button. The screen lights up. A swipe of her thumb wakes it fully.

The glow from her phone helps her spot the matchbook. She strikes one, melts the broken candle back together, waits for it to cool—then lights the wick.

She searches for a candle holder—can't remember ever owning one. A teacup will have to do. She drips wax into the bottom, then secures the candle upright.

She closes her phone and slips it into her pocket. Using her candle to light the way, she returns to the living room. She sets the candle on the mantle and builds a fire.

She can't believe it—she, a thriller writer, spooked by a little snow. She chuckles, tossing another log on the fire.

Warmth returns to the room. Wanting a clean pair of socks, she lifts her candle and heads for her bedroom—but freezes at the hallway.

A man stands in the bedroom doorway. His back is to her. Candlelight spills past him, illuminating just enough.

## What Happened to the Oranges?

In the twitch of his shoulders, she sees it. He knows he's been discovered.

She blows out the candle. He turns. She bolts—full throttle. Behind her, his footsteps close in fast.

Her breathing hitches in and out. Heart skips, stumbles, slams against her chest. She crashes into the kitchen—mind spinning. She hunts for a weapon?

The fire poker still sits in the puddle of melted snow near the backdoor. There are knives in the block on the counter.

Maybe she should hide.

She curses herself for choosing the kitchen. For buying a house with no hiding spots and owning too few weapons.

For acting like a victim in her own books.

She snatches up the fire poker and slides beneath the kitchen table, curling around it's legs like a shield.

Should've grabbed a knife instead. She still could—

—but then he enters, blocking her path to everything else.

She lets out an involuntary sound somewhere between a squeal and a groan. He freezes, listening for her. She catches her breath and holds it tightly.

She crouches, ready to lunge.

Poker in hand. Muscles coiled.

Jab, stab, strike—whatever it takes.

But he doesn't move. And neither can she.

"I know you came in here," he growls—a bite in his whisper.

Her heart pounds—surely loud enough to give her away.

He opens the door, peers into the night.

Her grip tightens. Could she rush him? Drive him out?

She summons her courage as he turns to face the table.

The door stands open, the moonlight spills in behind him—casting shadows that skitter across his face, sharpening every angle.

He smiles. A sneer. He's found her.

She gasps and starts scooting backward until her butt bumps against a table leg.

**Whoosh, schwump, splat.**

Snow crashes from the roof behind him.

He jumps. Turns.

This time, she doesn't flinch.

She lunges—poker first, like a spear.

It sinks into his side. She drives him backward, out the door.

She leaves the poker in him. Leaves him in the yard. Slams the door. Bolts it.

She sprints to the bathroom, slams the door, locks it. Climbs into the tub. Draws the curtain.

Phone in hand, she dials 911.

"911, what's the nature of your emergency?"

The operator answers just as the kitchen door splinters.

"There's a man in my house," she whispers from her flimsy shelter.

"What is your relationship to the man?"

## *What Happened to the Oranges?*

"I don't have a relationship with him," she hisses—the words burning her throat.

"You are reporting a male intruder?"

The operator's calm grates her nerves.

From the kitchen—crash. The table flips. Chairs tumble.

"Yes,"

"Can you safely leave the home?"

"Don't you think I would have already?" she growls, voice cracking with fury.

"There's no need to get angry. Officers have been dispatched to your location. They will be there just as soon as they can."

None of it reassures her.

He's crashing through the living room now.

She gulps air. The operator keeps talking.

The noise grows louder. Closer.

"Officers will be there soon."

She can't speak.

He found her. He's right outside the door.

She locked it, of course he knew she was there.

Stupid. So stupid.

He slams into the door.

She whimpers into the phone.

The operator's voice her only thread— "Hang on. Hang on."

"You called the cops!" he bellows angrily.

He pounds again.

The phone slips from her hand—clatters against porcelain.

## Tiffany Higgins

Then—

Nothing.

Not even her heartbeat.

Just stillness. So poignant it feels like the end.

*Am I dead?* She wonders.

"Police!" comes a shout outside the door.

She is too afraid to answer.

"Ma'am, if you're in there, it's safe to come out now."

She doesn't move. She doesn't make a sound. She holds her breath and waits.

"In here!" another voice shouts—

—and then the door splinters open.

She screams. Uniforms flood her vision—but they don't feel real. She can't stop screaming.

"Ma'am, it's alright. You're safe."

But the scream is louder than him

Louder than thought.

She's cracked—

and it's still spilling over.

# III.

Decisions, once made, can spiral out of control.

Tiffany Higgins

*What Happened to the Oranges?*

# THE MISCHIEF ECHOES

*We're all a part of something.*

🍊🍊🍊

Karina's day had already derailed, and it wasn't even lunchtime. Sanity was starting to feel like a distant memory. The lab was mostly deserted, just the way she liked it. She fancied herself a rogue lab rat, rising above the mischief. The chimpanzee she was working with was the closest thing she wanted to having a friend here at work.

She'd arrived early today, courtesy of a bus that, for the first time in recorded history, had shown up on schedule. Still groggy and in no mood for small talk with equally introverted coworkers, Karina stopped at the corner coffee cart. The barista didn't look up. Just scribbled, poured, passed her the cup like a secret agent.

The heat of the cup seeped into her chilled fingers. She sipped and watched the elevator numbers tick down. When the doors opened, a lab tech stepped in — Adam? Allen? One of those A names.

"It's Kevin," he said.

She blinked. "Excuse me?"

"My name. The one you couldn't remember." He never turned around.

Her mouth opened, a question half-formed —

—but the doors slid open, and she slipped past him without asking.

With a mental shrug and a quick sip of her coffee, she'd slipped past him off the elevator. She turned back.

"Kev—"

But the elevator was empty. The air still smelled like him.

Karina walked into the lab looking like she'd been sucking a lemon. She scanned the room—no Kevin. Not a trace. Whatever that had been, she could deal with it later. For now—work.

She powered on her dinosaur of a computer, then wandered off in search of last week's enzyme results. Maybe she'd left them near the salamander—the one she'd been chatting to while categorizing.

Kevin stood, motionless, in front of the salamander's cage. Eerily still.

"Hi, Kevin."

Nothing. Not even a muscle twitch.

"I'll just—yeah, I'm taking these." She grabbed the stack of papers.

She glanced back as the door shut.

Empty. No Kevin.

By the time she returned, the dinosaur had finished wheezing to life. Karina opened the spreadsheet. The screen blinked. Black. Then blue. Then purple.

## *What Happened to the Oranges?*

She furrowed her brow. The purple was beautiful—but wrong. Her computer had never glowed like that. She smacked the monitor. Clicked the mouse. Smacked it again.

Bright orange letters blazed across the screen.
GOODBYE.

Once. Twice. Three times. Then they collapsed inward, merging together, folding into a pinprick of light.

"Well, that's not good," she muttered.

She glanced around. She was alone.

Then the screen flickered—and played a time-lapse of a butterfly's metamorphosis. Repeat. Again and again.

Karina watched. Mesmerized.

Black, blue, purple. Then again:
GOODBYE.

Flashed three times. Merged. Gone.

Karina reached for the phone. Enough was enough.

She sipped her lukewarm coffee and wandered the halls of B-1. No chatter. No footsteps. No Kevin. Just empty labs and still air.

The elevator dinged. Karina returned to her desk just in time to meet tech support—who looked about twelve. Thick orange glasses. Button-up hanging off his shoulders. Baggy pants. Beat up sneakers. He resembled a child pretending to be a grown-up.

"I'm Jim. You got a computer you sayin' prayers or speakin' tongues?" His voice was a shock—deep, gravelly, like it came from someone twice his size.

"Yeah, I think it's possessed."

"Let's take a look."

She stepped aside. He leaned in, typing, grunting, muttering under his breath like he was decoding a spell.

"Any idea where everyone is?" Karina asked.

Jim didn't look up. "Probably at Kevin's funeral."

She blinked. "Kevin's what?"

The cold crept across her skin and seeped into her bones.

"Yeah," Jim said casually, still typing. "Kevin's the one who died in that car crash last week,"

Like it was old news.

She was a rogue lab rat, not a part of the mischief.

And that's how she'd hurt him. She hadn't shown up.

But Kevin had known where he'd find her: working.

*What Happened to the Oranges?*

# WAR ON FOREIGN SOIL

*Loyalty led him into battle, but he awoke amputated from the dream.*

I was a patriot because I was raised to be a patriot. I never questioned loyalty to my country. I never considered not loving my country.

I knew I would grow up to be a soldier. It was what my father had been. And his father before him. And so on and so forth for as many fathers as we could trace back through our family line.

I loved the calisthenics of gym class, so basic training was a breeze for me. I hadn't considered global tensions when I had enlisted on my eighteenth birthday. I had expected to spend my years marching around base and saying 'Yes, sir' a lot, just as my father had.

I was going to find me a pretty girl. If she could bake my grandma's banana bread with the toasted walnuts just the way I liked them, I might have even married her. We'd be a fixture in the community because everyone loved her as much as I do.

But those were just dreams. Dreams that were dashed by a war on foreign soil I never should have set foot on. The bluetooth navigation system led our convoy right into the enemy's hands.

## Tiffany Higgins

Instead of lying in bed beside a beautiful wife, I find myself here on this cold metal slab. The flimsy curtain that separates me from the rest of the room billows in an imagined breeze as I slip in and out of consciousness.

The words that float to me from the other side of that divide are foreign. I can't remember if I recognize them. I think I heard the word amputated or maybe it was carbonated.

The darkness closes in.

*What Happened to the Oranges?*

# THE VISITOR

*Some choices don't ask for permission.*

🍊🍊🍊

The card was black as pitch. The words Lesser of Two Evils were etched in gold and perfectly centered. I squinted my eyes, trying to read the fine print just beneath those words. I brought the card closer to my face, but the words remained unclear. I turned my attention to the man whose knock had brought me from the warmth and comfort of my kitchen.

He was an unassuming man; plain in both look and attire. His black suit jacket was buttoned. His white shirt was neatly pressed with just the right amount of starch in the collar which was folded over the charcoal gray tie he wore. His patent leather shoes had the perfect balance of dull shine.

Pale blue eyes peered out from beneath a black fedora. His peaches and cream skin had the texture of soft velvet. He was clean shaven. He appeared neither young nor old.

Despite the cold winter's day, he wore no overcoat. I couldn't see a car in the driveway, and I wondered how he'd ended up on my front stoop. I sensed neither malice nor kindness in him.

"Can I help you?" I asked, breaking the silence.

He handed me a magnifying glass. I held the card beneath the lens. "All will be revealed in time," it read.

"Can I help you?" I asked again.

His continued silence was unnerving. He held out his hand palm up. When I failed to comply, he indicated the magnifying glass that hung limply by my side and then held out his hand once more.

I set it gently on his flattened palm. He closed his fingers around it. The dirt and grime in his nails felt out of place. I looked at him again. His clothes were dirty, and the fabric had deteriorated in large patches. His shoes were scuffed and cracking.

His skin bore a bluish-gray hue and was dry and flaky. His pale blue eyes had grown paler as he stood there. He brought them slowly up to meet mine.

"Thank you," he whispered as he turned and walked off my porch.

*What Happened to the Oranges?*

# DAWN'S EARLY LIGHT

> *There are times when the nightmare is better than reality.*

🍊🍊🍊

Dawn approaches. I can see it in my peripheral. It's there, just out of sight. But I know it's there nonetheless.

I scribble my words down on a scrap of paper. I know that the dawn brings with it the stink of death. I can smell it there. Lurking on the other side of daylight. Just waiting for me to peek out from behind these curtains.

The stench of him crawls up my nose and takes up residence there. I feel my skin crawl and wonder if he's whispered my name yet.

I know it's coming. The dawn. The death. My death. It's a fantastic death. I've seen it in visions my entire life. I've always known it would end at this moment on this day.

I knew I would never reach twenty-one. People like me. Clairvoyants or whatever they call us these days. We just know. They can't explain it to us, and we can't explain it to them.

I've lived a good life. Well, as good as anyone can in twenty-odd years.

The sun ticks another notch into the sky. It's starting to just take the edge off of the darkness. Death lurks outside my door. I can hear him now. Panting and snarling. He's got a taste for me. He won't stop until he's had his fill.

He takes a deep breath in and I know he's smelling me. Sniffing the air for delicious morsels like one might do when there's fresh bread baking in the oven.

A shiver travels down my spine. I feel my body quake. I check the locks again. I know I'm powerless to stop this. I've seen it too many times to believe I can save myself.

I stayed awake all night. I barricaded the doors and locked down all the windows tight. I see the orange glow beginning just on the other side of my window blinds.

I begin to pray—not to one god but to many. I plead for any single one of them to step in. I swear loyalty if they'll just spare my life from this impending death.

The door rattles. The pounding comes next.

Rattle. Pound. Rattle. Pound.

I hear my name. It chooses my mother's voice.

Rattle. Pound. Pound. Rattle.

Mom calls my name again.

The smell of bacon wafts in from the hallway. It feels fitting that Mom's cooking bacon for my final day.

"Time to wake up. It's a school day," Mom shouts from the other side of my bedroom door. The sun rises higher.

"I'm not going," I shout, pulling the blanket over my head. "I'm going back to sleep."

# IV.

Moments of hope, strength, and compassion.

Tiffany Higgins

## IN THE WOODS

> *She came for rest—but the woods can be exhilarating.*

I came to a stop in the gravel driveway. I'd finally arrived. Somehow, I'd managed to swing that vacation I'd been dreaming of.

The quaint little cottage stood just inside the edge of a beautiful old forest. The trees stood tall and majestic against the setting sun. Their leaves glinted like diamonds in hues of green and blue. The thick trunks were more shades of brown than I'd ever known.

I felt a peaceful calm wash over me in their presence. I grabbed my duffel and laptop from the backseat. I slipped the key from my pocket as I headed toward the door.

The old steps creaked beneath my feet as I climbed them. The cottage's white paint had grayed with age. It was chipped and peeled. It had a lovingly lived-in look rather than one of neglect.

The key turned easily enough in the recently oiled locks. The knob groaned when I turned it, and the hinges creaked in protest as the door swung open.

I blinked into the darkening space beyond the door. I fumbled along the wall for a light switch. I found none.

In the dusky light, I could just make out the shape of a small lamp atop an equally small table. It stood just steps away. I fumbled beneath the shade for the switch.

The lamp cast pale yellow light across the room. A small but plush sofa sat in the center of the room. It was adorned in silky upholstery dotted with tiny pink rosebuds. A matching chair sat at an angle slightly wider than ninety degrees from the right arm of the couch. An oval table with an array of magazines was set askew in front of them.

I found a tall lamp tucked into the corner of the room. It cast a milky hue to everything. The yellow light turned the sickening shade of a tornado-brewing sky. I turned off the small lamp. The milky hue brightened.

The cottage was sparce. The kitchen stood against one wall which was separated from the main space by a narrow island counter. Two stools had been placed at the small counter.

Against the far corner stood a small stove. Then came a strip of counter, a small sink, and then another strip of counter. A small refrigerator with rounded corners and a freezer cabinet hidden inside was tucked into the other corner.

Above the sink was a rather large window with a perfect view of the woods beyond. On either side of the window hung small kitchen cabinets. I'd been a bit surprised when the leasing agent had offered to stock the kitchen, but the cabinets and fridge had been fully stocked with the groceries I'd requested.

## *What Happened to the Oranges?*

A glass percolator was set on a back burner of the stove. Coffee was exactly what I needed after the long drive, so I set it to brew. When the stove wouldn't light, I began to worry a bit, but I soon located a tin full of matches and had a small flame burning in no time.

While the coffee percolated, I set off to explore the rest of the cottage. Across the small main room stood a wall with three doors.

The door on the left opened to reveal a small bathroom done up in peaches and cream with small shells as the main decor. On the right was a clawfoot tub with a transparent shower curtain encircling it. The shower head was attached directly to a pipe jutting from a hole in the wall.

To the left were a toilet and a small pedestal sink. A medicine cabinet with a mirror hung above. Though it barely fit, a shell-shaped peach bathmat was tucked into the space between the tub and the sink.

I opened the next door to find a closet stocked full of linens. A stick vacuum leaned in the corner. There were a few bars of hand soap, a spare bottle of dish soap, and a stack of paperbacks. Planning to check out the titles later, I closed the door and reached for the third knob.

The bedroom wasn't as small as I had expected it to be. It wasn't as large as the one I shared with my husband back home, but it was a comfortable space. The four-poster, full-sized bed was topped with a plush mattress. It was draped in a powder blue duvet over cornflower blue sheets. Everything was trimmed with delicate lace.

A small oak nightstand with a tiny drawer was set on either side of the bed. A brass lamp hung on the wall above each. A long oak dresser that matched the nightstands stood against the wall. After catching a glimpse of my reflection in the large oval mirror adorning the dresser, I promised to shower before climbing into the inviting bed.

The smell of coffee was starting to permeate the air, so I turned off the stove. The sun had finished setting as I took my cup–heavily laden with sugar and cream–and settled back on the sofa cushions.

It had been a long drive. I was exhausted. I finished my drink, rinsed the cup, and left it in the sink to be washed in the morning. After a quick shower, I crawled into bed. I was thinking about a hike into those beautiful woods as I drifted off to sleep.

I had such bizarre dreams that night. A man called to me from the woods. A woman cried for help. The trees told me: trust no one. The man begged me to come with him. The woman screamed in agony. The trees whispered their dire warnings. I awoke feeling well-rested. Though most would probably feel uneasy, my dreams did nothing to warn me off from my hike in the woods. I ate a couple of muffins warmed in the oven and drank entirely too much coffee, same as every morning.

## *What Happened to the Oranges?*

I found a cute little picnic basket on top of the fridge. I put together a picnic lunch; a sandwich, potato salad, a thick slice of chocolate cake, and a bottle of iced tea. I dressed in jeans and a warm sweater. I slipped on a pair of comfortable hiking boots. After I secured my hair in a ponytail, I grabbed my packed basket and slipped out the door, which I left unlocked in spite of the key in my pocket.

The cooler temperatures had arrived the previous week; just in time for my well-deserved vacation. The air smelled crisp and fresh. The true arrival of fall was still weeks away, and very few leaves were tipped with autumnal colors yet. I thought I smelled a hint of rain, but the sky was blue without a cloud in sight.

I walked slowly at first, enjoying the sights and smells of nature untouched around me. I examined mosses on the trees and patches of mushrooms near their roots. I listened to the songbirds singing and the answering buzz of insects. The air smelled lush and green. I felt energized and excited.

Soon, I was skipping along the paths carved naturally between the trees. The animals tittered and tutted as they watched me frolic. I got the distinct impression that some were even laughing at me.

The trees shook out their long branches as they joined in my jubilee. I broke out into a song as though I'd been singing it my whole life. I knew every word though I'd never heard it before. It both comforted and alarmed me.

I stumbled into a clearing. It was a carpet of green grass and purple violets. A family of bunnies nibbled on the tender stalks. I did my best not to disturb them as I spread the small blanket out. I folded my arms behind my head as I lay across it. My backside hung over the edge, and I bent my knees in an attempt to keep it off the damp ground.

I closed my eyes and felt the warm rays of sunshine wash over my face. A curious young bunny sniffed at my ear. I held perfectly still and enjoyed the shared moment. I think I drifted off for a bit.

When I awoke, I was famished. I sat up; making sure my bottom was planted on the blanket. I unpacked my lunch and devoured it with a hunger I was unfamiliar with. I attributed it to the fresh air I seldom got in my everyday life.

I looked around the field. The bunnies had abandoned me, and I found myself alone. Clouds had moved in, and the brightness of the day had dulled. Across the field, the trees were scrawny and barren. A single path snaked between the desolate-looking trunks.

Curious, I abandoned my blanket to follow it. I had barely started down the path when I came upon a set of iron steps that led to an iron door. The door swung open invitingly.

Inside, I could see a perfect wood. The trees were lush and full of bright green leaves. There were large, thick bushes in the distance. The path that led through the door continued beyond it. I could see a beautiful castle against a summer sky backdrop. I hesitated there at the precipice.

I considered the path in front of me before glancing back where I'd come from. I took a step backward, examining the door further. I saw something in my peripheral vision. Had that tree just moved?

"Come…" a whisper came from the other side.

I squinted, searching for movement. There. That tree—were those eyes?

"What are you waiting for?" The whisper crawled up my skin.

The tree was grinning at me then. Have you ever seen a tree grin? It's the most unnerving thing to see a tree spread its leaves into an eerie grimace.

I slammed that iron door so hard it echoed through the woods like a gunshot. I turned and ran down the stairs and through the trees back to the clearing. I scooped up the blanket and basket as I ran across the field of purple and green.

I picked the path I thought was most likely to lead me back to my little vacation cottage. Only when my lungs began to feel like they would burst did I slow to a walk.

The path seemed long as the sky changed to shades of orange and purple. I could barely drag my feet when the cottage finally came into view.

I was so glad I hadn't locked the door as I tumbled through it and then turned and collapsed against it. I secured the lock and sat in a heap on the floor.

## Tiffany Higgins

In my busy city life, I had forgotten how a walk in the woods could be equal parts invigorating, exhilarating, and exhausting.

*What Happened to the Oranges?*

# CHOCOLATE SUNDAE, NO TOMATO

*Love will find a way.*

🍊🍊🍊

There she was, across the room. Beauty and grace in motion. Her soft, brunette waves were secured by a clip, and though he couldn't see them from where he stood, he knew her electric green eyes sparkled with merriment.

He remembered the first time he'd seen her. There were no any customers, so he'd been working on trying to convince the boss to give him a rare Friday night off despite the lack of notice. The bell above the door had chimed, and they'd both turned to look.

New in town and in need of a job, she'd walked in, grabbed the **NOW HIRING** sign out of the window, slapped it down on the counter, and declared, "Your search is over."

Of course, the boss had hired her. She'd have been a fool not to. All that moxie and confidence rolled into one pretty package. Arline had started the very next day, and Billy had been glad that the boss had denied him the night off.

Billy had wanted so badly to go over and talk to her, but she was so beautiful, too beautiful for the likes of him. He was plain. Boring. He kept his brown hair cropped in a safe, boring cut. And his brown eyes were like every other pair of brown eyes out there.

Over the last few months since she'd started at the diner, they'd become friends. Though he was sure he was more than halfway in love with her, he hadn't gotten up the nerve to ask her out.

He leaned against the wall, an unlit cigarette dangling from his lips, and watched her. She was the perfect blend of curves and padding. Her body moved like life was a dance.

Arline flounced from table to table, expertly filling cups and clearing dishes as she wrote down orders and delivered food. With a wink and a smile, she always delivered impeccable service. She earned a generous tip from even the thriftiest customer.

A slow smile crept across his lips as she sauntered towards him, hips swaying to a beat uniquely hers. She smiled at him. A genuine smile. A wide smile. A beautiful smile.

"Hey, Billy." He loved the way his name rolled off her tongue. "Let me get four house specials—all day—and a kiddie's chicken and French fries—absolutely no yucky tomato."

"No tomato?" He wrinkled his brow in confusion.

"That adorable little blonde girl at table seven made me promise I'd tell the cook 'Absaloolee no yucky tomato,' and so I am."

He peeked at the girl at table seven. She was four or five years old with a sweet cherub face flushed a pale pink and surrounded by pale blonde curls. Adorable didn't begin to

## What Happened to the Oranges?

describe her. He slid the cigarette behind his ear as he pushed off the wall.

"I never could deny a pretty girl anything."

In the kitchen, he dropped the fries and tenders into the fryer and pushed the appropriate buttons. He slapped four frozen halibut filets on the grill. As they began to sizzle, he grabbed the house salads from the fridge and set them in the window, lingering just long enough to watch her grab them and walk away.

Inside his head, he practiced asking her out over and over again while he set the plates. He flipped the fish. He scooped and smoothed a bed of herbaceous rice on four of the five plates. He made a lettuce bed on the fifth.

The timers went off on both the tenders and the fries. Billy shook the baskets before hanging them to drip. The sizzling had slowed, and he knew the halibut had finished. He placed a filet on each bed of rice. He dumped the fries and tenders onto the lettuce bed. Each plate received a scoop of the daily vegetable.

"Order up!" he announced as he set the plates in the window.

Sway, swish, sashay—smile, wink. Her walk was a slow dance, and he longed to dance it with her. Mesmerized and hypnotized by the gentle sway of her hips, he forgot he was staring. He stood, mouth agape, as she loaded her tray.

"Whatchya need, honey?" Her words brought him back to himself.

"Huh, what? Oh, sorry. Guess I was kinda spaced out or something. I'm gonna take out the trash and grab a smoke. You be all right a minute?"

"Yeah, yeah. I got this. You go ahead."

Billy watched through the window as she sashayed her way to table seven. When Arline set her plate down, the little girl protested.

"I didn't order no vegables."

Arline glanced over her shoulder and winked at him.

"Cook said if you eat all your vegetables, there's a free dessert in it for you."

"What kinda dessert?" She'd piqued the girl's interest.

"You'll have to eat your vegetables to find out."

"I hope it's a chocolate sundae. I'll eat my whole dinner, even the lettuce, for a chocolate sundae."

She shrugged vaguely at the girl. "Cook didn't tell me."

Satisfied that the matter was resolved, she turned and delivered the remaining daily specials to the only other table in the diner. An elderly couple who'd watched the entire exchange with gentle smiles alighting their faces.

He grabbed the garbage and slipped out the kitchen door. He heard her asking them if there was anything else she could get for them. After he'd tossed the bag into the dumpster, Billy paced back and forth in the chilly night air, puffing on his cigarette.

## What Happened to the Oranges?

"Arline," he said to the empty alley. "I've been thinking that maybe... No. Don't say maybe." He took another puff off his cigarette. "I've been wondering... Yeah, wondering." He dropped his cigarette and snuffed it out with the toe of his boot. "Aw hell, just say it. Arline, would you go out with me?"

"Yes!" she squealed from the kitchen door where she'd stood unseen. "I thought you'd never ask me."

Arline burst out of the doorway and came running at him full tilt. She threw her arms around his neck and planted her lips on his. It was a sweet, tender kiss that tasted faintly of bubble gum. He slid his arms around her waist and pulled her closer, deepening the kiss. They were both panting when they came up for air.

"As much as I want to keep doing that," she said, planting one more quick kiss on his lips. "Right now, you owe a little girl who ate all her dinner—even the lettuce—a chocolate sundae."

She took his hand, and they returned to work together.

# Tiffany Higgins

*What Happened to the Oranges?*

## TWO STUFFIES WALK INTO A BAR

> *Stuffies have stories. Sometimes they need comfort.*

It had taken my little human twice as long as usual to fall asleep after the excitement—and sugar buzz—of the birthday party. I finally escaped from my drooling friend and made my way to the local stuffie's bar. I signaled the barkeep for a beer and plopped into the seat beside my friend.

"You won't believe the day I've had."

He laughed a harsh, barking laugh. "The day you've had? Wait until I tell you about the day I've had." Raising his glass, he signaled the barkeep to bring him another. He was already getting a little loud.

"Alright, alright. Settle down." The waitress set down two mugs and smiled at my rumpled friend.

She was an older bunny—well-loved with her stuffing all lumpy. It was obvious she'd been dragged around the playground in her day. Her little human was long since grown. Nobody was looking for her anymore.

I paid her, returned her smile, and added a generous tip. I promised I wouldn't get nearly as drunk as my friend probably would. She laughed, and it was melodic and soothing. My friend relaxed beside me, and I took a long sip of cool beer.

"Alright," I said when he remained quiet and brooding. "Why don't you go first?"

"Nah. You had 'a day,' right? Go on, let's hear it." He took a slug of beer.

"Richy had a birthday party today. His first sleepover."

"That was your first sleepover too, wasn't it?"

"Yes. How come you never told me about them?"

"Something you had to experience for yourself, friend."

"Experience it, I did."

"Sounds like maybe you did have quite the day." He settled back in his seat, more relaxed now, and sipped his beer.

"At first Richy clung to me like he always has when he's scared. He clung to my foot and carried me through the door with my head bouncing off of his leg. His backpack was slung over his shoulder, and it weighed him down. It gave him a lean, and my ear scraped on the floor. He followed his friend into a big room full of boys. It was noisy—boys screaming, shouting, laughing. It seemed like everyone had brought their stuffie, and it was going to be a fun old time. I was feeding off the excitement and ready to make new friends."

"It's always good to make friends with your fellow hostages."

I choked on the swig of beer. I couldn't suppress my laughter at being called a hostage. I wish somebody had thought to negotiate my release.

"Yes, well, about those fellow hostages. By the time I showed up, crabbiness was spreading through the ranks. One particular

## What Happened to the Oranges?

penguin was feeling especially mean-spirited. I saw him shove a unicorn into the couch."

He gave me that look. The one that said, "Your head is full of stuffing."

"I see that look on your face. You don't believe me. But I saw him shove that unicorn down into the couch, behind the cushions. The birthday boy's little sister cried and cried. She couldn't find her missing 'uneecrone', and she swore that somebody had stolen it. When they finally pulled her up, she was barely breathing. I told her if she made her way up here I'd buy her a drink, but the poor thing will likely be recovering for days."

"Well, I'll be. I ain't never seen a stuffie try to commit stuffiecide at a party before. Did the penguin belong to the birthday boy? Was there a sibling-type rivalry between them?'

"No! The penguin was there with a guest. And he wasn't acting like a guest should act at all."

"Did he belong to a rotten child?"

"No again. The boy he came with was a shy, quiet kind of boy. I got the impression that the penguin wasn't his usual stuffie and maybe it wasn't used to being out of the house."

"Well, that can be enough to make any stuffie misbehave. Do you remember your first time out?"

"I had it easy. I went to the grocery store. Sat in the cart with Richy the whole time."

"I went to the park. Matilda dragged me through the sandbox. Then, she buried me in it. I had to go straight to the wash when we got home. Tildy cried and cried all night for me."

He sipped his beer, and I swear—a single tear trickled down his cheek.

"Well get on with it then. Tell me your story," he said.

"Richy kept me in hand as he ran and jumped and screamed with his friends. They played all kinds of wild games. Then, they decided to have a stuffie fight."

"Oh no, they didn't." I heard somebody gasp from behind me. I turned around to find a silver-furred beauty sitting on the edge of her seat listening to my tale. Her golden eyes searched mine, begging for me to continue.

"They did. They grabbed us by whatever body parts they could wrap their little fingers around, and they swung us at each other with all their might. Like we were weapons in some crazy war."

"My Samantha would never do that to me." The silver beauty swore, but her voice quivered.

"My Richy swung me on his friend so hard I knocked him to the ground. Then he held me up to take the blow from somebody swinging a horse at his head. And before I could even catch my breath, he swung me back 'round on the birthday boy who deflected the blow with his own rather large teddy bear."

"So… did you win?"

## *What Happened to the Oranges?*

"I didn't win anything. I was flung from Richy's hands. I was sent spinning round and round until I slammed into the wall—nothing more than a crumpled heap."

"Oh, you poor thing," Silver said as she stood and sauntered over to our table.

"That ain't nothing," my drunken friend shouted a bit belligerently. "Nothin' at all compared to the day I've had." He slammed the rest of his beer and rudely demanded another.

Silver slid a hand down my furry cheek. The touch felt good. I leaned into it. I didn't usually hook up at the bar. But it had been a long night.

"Alright. Enough. Tell me what the hell's wrong with you," I said.

"Matilda's gone. Moved out."

"What do you mean 'moved out'?"

"She moved somewhere else. Left me behind sitting on the bed."

"But Tildy would never do that. She loves you."

"Apparently not as much as she loves *Brian*." He said the name like it tasted disgusting.

"Oh, Buddy. She'll remember how much she needs you and come back to find you before you know it."

"You really think so?" He sniffled.

"Of course I do."

His dark brown fur was matted in places and bare in others. Matilda had loved him. She'd taken him everywhere with her–

even to college. I wondered how she could have left him behind so easily now.

"Why don't you finish telling us about that birthday party," he said sounding a little more at ease again.

"I lay there, discarded, until bedtime. Richy snatched me up in his sticky hands–no one had made him wash or brush his teeth–and settled down into his sleeping bag. He pulled me snug against his face drowning me in all the sugary drool and cake crumbs. Once I was certain he was sound asleep, I pulled myself from his grip—came up here for a cold draft."

"And I'm so glad you did." Silver cooed at me as she leaned in closer.

"I'm flattered, really—I am." I lied. She'd lost her appeal. "But my friend here needs me tonight. So, I'm going to have to ask that you find somewhere else to hang." I removed her paws from around me.

She pouted but wasted no time arguing. She found a green fox at the bar and started putting the moves on him.

"Aw, you didn't have to go and do a thing like that. I'll be just fine with my beer. You should go do something crazy with that silver-furred beauty before you let your whole life pass you by without ever taking a chance, doing something crazy— something that might make a little girl cry when she can't find you before the school bus comes."

## What Happened to the Oranges?

"Don't talk like that. I've seen you do plenty of crazy things right here in this very bar including that purple gorilla who couldn't keep his paws off you."

He smiled at the memory. "See. You need memories like that, too."

"Not with her." I rolled my eyes.

"Fine. Just promise me you'll make your own wild memories with a stuffie that can't get enough of you one day, too."

"Sun's coming up soon. Time to return to the human world. Off ya go now," the barkeep shouted.

"Don't worry," he said as we stood up from our table. "Your little human won't be awake for hours. Sugar buzzes crash hard. That drooling mess you left little Richy in? That's what I mean. He'll feel kinda crappy when he wakes up and likely wanna snuggle you closer. He might even take a nap when he gets home."

"I'll keep that in mind. Thanks."

"Oh and." He sniffed the air. "His mom's likely gonna wanna give you a wash."

"Yeah. I figured as much."

"See you next time."

"Yeah, you too. And Tildy's gonna come back for you. Just you watch and see."

"Or maybe she'll leave Brian and come back home."

"Maybe she will." I smiled at him. "Bye."

"Bye."

## Tiffany Higgins

I turned and walked back to the slumber party, into the arms of the sleeping boy I loved so much.

*What Happened to the Oranges?*

## ON THE TIP OF THE TONGUE

*Some words don't get lost. They get stranded.*

One job, man. You had one job.

Spit me out. That's all you had to do.

Now, I'm stuck—right here on the tip of your tongue.

It's a bit dry here, by the way. Maybe that cool glass of water—sitting there beside your hand—could have helped.

If you had simply taken a moment to take a sip, then I would be out there surfing with my friends across those radical sound waves.

But, no. You were too nervous to take that drink. Afraid you'd spill it all over the front of that pressed shirt. Afraid you'd make a mess.

Make a mess you did, didn't you? You can feel all those words backing up behind me, can't you? The way they're stumbling over each other trying to get out.

They aren't getting past me though. Nope. We are all stuck here because you are too stubborn to take a sip of water.

You're starting to choke on them now. Those words clogging your throat. Those words that should have surfed into your audience's brainwaves?

## Tiffany Higgins

They haunt you now—when it was your audience you meant to haunt.

Oh, sure. Now you're going to take that drink of water. Now, it's too late. You're just going to *glub… glub… glub…*

## WHAT HAPPENED TO THE ORANGES?

*Compassion breeds mercy.*

🍊🍊🍊

We sat in hard plastic chairs in front of the boss's desk. He leaned back—expression unreadable, hands folded across his ample stomach.

"Alright. Tell me how it happened."

"Well, it was like this," I began. "I watched the box fall in slow motion. It tumbled. It flipped. It spilled. Oranges rolled—bright and colorful—in every direction.

"That's when I realized we were parked at the top of a hill. The oranges, they just kept on rolling. They rolled down the hill and into traffic. Some wound up under passing car tires. It became a pulpy, juicy mess that just kept getting worse."

"Why'd'ya hafta go n tell 'im it was me that dropped them oranges?" Jim interrupted me.

"What are ya talkin' about? I didn't say you dropped the box."

"Well, ya said ya watched it happen. N that means it was me who done it."

"I didn't tell him no such thing—but you just did."

Jim buried his face in his hands. Nothing he could do now. The boss knew for sure who'd caused the juicy, pulpy mess back on the road.

To our surprise, the boss burst into laughter—big, booming bellyfuls that shook the walls. His face turned an angry red, almost purple, as he gasped for breath.

We sat silent and unmoving in those uncomfortable chairs, waiting to be fired. But the firing never came.

"Get on back to work, boys," he wheezed between gasps as the laughter subsided.

"Yes, sir!" we answered in unison, springing to our feet.

Neither of us said another word. Relief flooded us with endorphins as we practically ran to the truck.

*What Happened to the Oranges?*

## ABOUT TIFFANY

Tiffany Higgins writes for those who know how silence aches and how stories can speak louder than words. Her work blends emotional truth with advocacy, often exploring the spaces where systems fail—and people choose to rise anyway.
Whether she's unraveling myth, memory, or quiet defiance, Tiffany's stories reflect a deep belief in resilience, integrity, and the dignity of being heard.
She lives in Michigan with her family and a small crew of cats, dreaming up ways to turn storytelling into a kind of shelter—for others and for herself.

Tiffany Higgins

*What Happened to the Oranges?*

# MORE BY TIFFANY HIGGINS

🍊🍊🍊

If *What Happened to the Oranges?* moved you, there's more to explore across genres and ages—stories that speak softly, challenge boldly, and resonate deeply.

### BOOKS AVAILABLE IN PRINT AND KINDLE EDITIONS:

### Love Sick: Stories

An anthology that explores love in all its forms—romantic, platonic, parental, and unrequited. From whimsical worlds to quiet heartbreaks, each tale invites reflection on how love shapes us in unexpected ways.

### Child Eater

In this haunting debut novel, a small town wrestles with legend and loss as a child disappears—and history threatens to repeat itself. Dark, atmospheric, and emotionally charged.

### Bully Troubles

A gentle tale of friendship, courage, and kindness. When Stone the cat faces unfair bullying, he and Bear B must find strength without losing compassion. Includes activities and accessible formatting for young readers.

# Tiffany Higgins

## *PICTURE BOOKS IN PRINT*

### Monster Beneath My Bed
A suspenseful but comforting bedtime story for little ones learning to face nighttime worries. Perfect for read-aloud moments and cozy reassurance.

### I Love the Changing Seasons
Winner of the 2013 KART Kids Book List Award. A rhyming celebration of nature's rhythm and beauty through vibrant watercolor illustrations.

### We've Seen Santa
A magical Christmas adventure through playful verse and warm illustrations, following two siblings determined to spot Santa on Christmas Eve.

**Explore all of Tiffany's titles on Amazon.**

*What Happened to the Oranges?*

Made in the USA
Monee, IL
19 August 2025